God Culture For Kids
Why Do People Die?

God Culture For Kids
Why Do People Die?

© 2015 John A. Naphor

Published in New York, New York, by Morgan James Publishing. Morgan James and The Entrepreneurial Publisher are trademarks of Morgan James, LLC.
www.MorganJamesPublishing.com

The Morgan James Speakers Group can bring authors to your live event. For more information or to book an event visit The Morgan James Speakers Group at www.TheMorganJamesSpeakersGroup.com.

A **free** eBook edition is available with the purchase of this print book.

ISBN 9781630472641   paperback
ISBN 9781630472658   eBook
ISBN 9781630472665   hardcover
Library of Congress Control Number:
2014940587

CLEARLY PRINT YOUR NAME ABOVE IN UPPER CASE

Instructions to claim your free eBook edition:
1. Download the BitLit app for Android or iOS
2. Write your name in **UPPER CASE** on the line
3. Use the BitLit app to submit a photo
4. Download your eBook to any device

Cover Design by:
Chris Treccani
www.3dogdesign.net

Interior Design by:
Chris Treccani
www.3dogdesign.net

In an effort to support local communities, raise awareness and funds, Morgan James Publishing donates a percentage of all book sales for the life of each book to Habitat for Humanity Peninsula and Greater Williamsburg.

Get involved today, visit
www.MorganJamesBuilds.com

Habitat
for Humanity®
Peninsula and
Greater Williamsburg
Building Partner

GOD CULTURE FOR KIDS

FOR KIDS

Why Do People Die?

John A. Naphor

NEW YORK

In the beginning of time,
God created the whole world.

On Earth, God planted a garden, the Garden of Eden. Then God caused everything to live there. He made the plants and He made the animals. Most importantly, God made two people, Adam and Eve.

Life in the garden was perfect for Adam and Eve. They had everything they needed. They had plenty of food, clean water, and most importantly, they had each other.

Every day, God came to visit them in the garden. God loved Adam and Eve more than anything He had made. To keep them safe, He gave them one rule.

Adam and Eve were allowed to have anything they wanted in the garden. They could eat from any tree, they could play with any animal, and they could live anywhere they chose.

The one thing they could not do was eat from the tree of the knowledge of good and evil. God said that if they did, they would die.

One day Adam and Eve met someone very
bad. He came to them in the form of a snake
and he played a trick on them. He told them
to disobey God and eat from the tree of the
knowledge of good and evil.

At first, they questioned him. They told him that God said they were not allowed to do that. But Satan told them they would not die. Adam and Eve believed him and ate the bad fruit.

As soon as they did, Adam and Eve felt different.
They felt guilty and ashamed of disobeying God.
They felt . . . bad.

In all their time in God's beautiful garden, never before had Adam and Eve felt bad. Even worse, they began to do bad things.

Now that they had eaten the fruit, Adam and Eve had changed in a way that meant that people could now be bad, and do bad things. This was not good, because in God's garden nothing ever died. If God allowed Adam and Eve to stay, they would live forever, and so would their children and all the Earth's people for the rest of time. Imagine a world where all the bad people lived forever.

God still loved them, so He would not let this happen. He made Adam and Eve leave the Garden of Eden.

Since they could no longer eat from the good trees of the garden, especially a tree called the tree of life, Adam and Eve now started to die. All the people in the world who came after Adam and Eve would die one day, too.

But God was not mad at Adam and Eve.
He still loved them. He still wanted to give
them, and all people, a way to live forever.

So God made Heaven. Heaven is a place where people's souls can live forever, even after their bodies have died. But people cannot get there by themselves. They need help.

God sent His Son Jesus, who could also die, to help us. Our faith in Him takes away any badness, called sin, that lives inside of us. Without death, Jesus could not bring us home to Heaven.

When we get to Heaven we will live forever with God, and our friends and family, in the most beautiful city ever, the brand New Jerusalem. Even though our bodies die, we get to have the gift of everlasting life.

Printed in the USA
CPSIA information can be obtained
at www.ICGtesting.com
JSHW060043150824
68134JS00028B/2618